12/16/10

W9-BVU-369

GO NICKELODEON
GO DIEGO GO!™

Be Good, Bobos!

adapted by Erica David
based on the screenplay "The Bobos' Mother's Day"
written by Valerie Walsh
illustrated by Art Mawhinney

Ready-to-Read

Simon Spotlight/Nickelodeon
New York   London   Toronto   Sydney

Based on the TV series *Go, Diego, Go!*™ as seen on Nick Jr.®

SIMON SPOTLIGHT

An imprint of Simon & Schuster Children's Publishing Division

1230 Avenue of the Americas, New York, New York 10020

For information about special discounts for bulk purchases, please contact Simon & Schuster Special Sales at 1-866-506-1949 or business@simonandschuster.com.

Manufactured in the United States of America

0410 LAK

2 4 6 8 10 9 7 5 3

Library of Congress Cataloging-in-Publication Data

David, Erica.

Be good, Bobos! / adapted by Erica David ; based on the teleplay written by Valerie Walsh. — 1st ed.

p. cm. — (Ready-to-read)

"Based on the TV series Go, Diego, Go! as seen on Nick Jr."—Copyright p.

ISBN 978-1-4169-9539-5

I. Walsh, Valerie. II. Go, Diego, go! (Television program) III. Title.

PZ7.D28197Be 2010

[E]—dc22

2009014355

Hi! I am 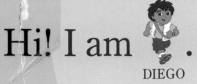.
DIEGO

Say hello to the .
BOBO BROTHERS

The 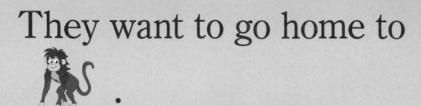 need our help.

BOBO BROTHERS

They want to go home to

 .

MOMMY BOBO

They want to be good

and not get into any trouble.

Look!

Do you see the  ?
TREE FROGS

The TREE FROGS are stuck in sap!

"Uh-oh! This is our fault," say the .

BOBO BROTHERS

"We are sorry, ."

TREE FROGS

The  want to give
TREE FROGS

their mommy a 🌸.
FLOWER

The 🐵🐵 can
BOBO BROTHERS

get the 🌸.
FLOWER

Good job, !
BOBO BROTHERS

Now the  have
TREE FROGS

a 🎁 for their mommy.
GIFT

Look!

Do you see  ?

SAMMY

cannot find any rainbow .

SAMMY   NUTS

"Uh-oh! This is our fault,"

say the .

BOBO BROTHERS

"We are sorry, 🐒."

SAMMY

 **SAMMY** wants to give the 🌰 **NUTS**

to his mommy.

The 🐵🐵 **BOBO BROTHERS** can

gather the 🌰 **NUTS**.

Good job, !
BOBO BROTHERS

Now  has a
SAMMY

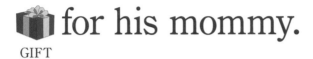 for his mommy.
GIFT

Look!

Do you see  ?
BABY JAGUAR

is sliding
BABY JAGUAR

on .
BANANA PEELS

"Uh-oh! This is our fault,"

say the .

BOBO BROTHERS

"We are sorry,  ."

BABY JAGUAR

The can

clean up the  .

Good job, !

BOBO BROTHERS

Now can go and

BABY JAGUAR

give his mommy a !

GIFT

The  want to give a .

BOBO BROTHERS

MOMMY BOBO

GIFT

 MOMMY BOBO likes  FLOWERS ,

 NUTS , and  BANANAS .

Do you see a  GIFT

for  MOMMY BOBO ?

Yeah,  !
BANANAS

The BOBO BROTHERS can give

BANANAS to MOMMY BOBO .

Now the  have

BOBO BROTHERS

a 🎁 for 🐒 !

GIFT MOMMY BOBO

The  give

BOBO BROTHERS

 her .

MOMMY BOBO   GIFT

 hugs her boys.

MOMMY BOBO

"We were very good today,"

say the .

BOBO BROTHERS

 smiles proudly.

MOMMY BOBO

"Thank you for the ,"

BANANAS

she says.

"But my boys being good

is the best  GIFT

a mommy could have!"